The Untold Sto
Itsy Bitsy's
Long, Emotional Day

JILL LEIBOWITZ, PSY.D.

where words connect

The Untold Story of Itsy Bitsy's Long, Emotional Day

First edition
(Paperback) ISBN: 978-1-946274-41-0
(e-book) ISBN: 978-1-946274-42-7
Library of Congress Control Number: 2020941822
[2 3 4 5 6 7 8 9 10]

Cover Photo:	Dominick Auciello
Cover Photo Editing:	Natalie Caricato
Cover and Interior Design:	Amit Dey
Illustrations:	Sunny Goel

Published by Wordeee in the United States, Beacon, New York 2020
Website: www.wordeee.com
Twitter and Facebook
e-mail: contact@wordeee.com

DEDICATION

For all the little spiders who've inspired me with their journeys down, and back up, the waterspout, especially my own, Oliver and Sadie.

For my husband, Dominick…I wouldn't want anyone else on my team.

For my father, Ron, who left our world before he could see this book and whose spirit lives on in its pages.

Itsy Bitsy ran with all her might, but the heavy rainwater created several waterways that roared like rapids through the garden.

On and on she sprinted for what must have been a million hours. And then, with a suddenness that surprised her, the yellow shoe bumped into a hydrangea bush.

But as she looked around, she realized that she had never seen this hydrangea bush before. In fact, she had never seen this part of the garden before. Was this even her garden?

Where was she? And where was Mama?

They searched and searched for that missing yellow shoe. Itsy Bitsy and Mama were exhausted. Mama sighed.

Itsy Bitsy felt sad and defeated.
She LOVED those yellow shoes.

Itsy Bitsy felt hopeless. And that's when Mama hugged her and came up with a solution.

Mama always knew exactly what to do. Wrapped in the safety of Mama's embrace, Itsy Bitsy felt so relieved she almost cried. But she held back her tears because she wanted to look brave and grown up. Mama would take her to Shoe Store Galore to buy a new set of her favorite yellow shoes. Hooray for Mama!

By now it was getting late, and they had to hurry to get to the store before it closed for the day. They were in such a rush, they even forgot to eat lunch.

Shoe Store Galore

Shoe Store Galore

Itsy Bitsy explored aisle after aisle. After what must have been a million hours...

14

Itsy Bitsy was so excited as she waited for the sales-spider to bring her eight of the most wonderful yellow shoes in the whole wide world. She imagined showing off this brand new set of shoes to all her friends tomorrow.

17

SAD? Mama did not understand. Something deep inside Itsy Bitsy began to grow.

Her face felt hot.

Her stomach felt hungry.

Her body felt tired.

It had been a long, emotional day.

19

The thing inside her grew bigger. It was heavy SAD that she couldn't have her yellow shoes. It was smashing MAD at Mama for everything bad that happened today. It was gigantic SCARED that these feelings would never go away.

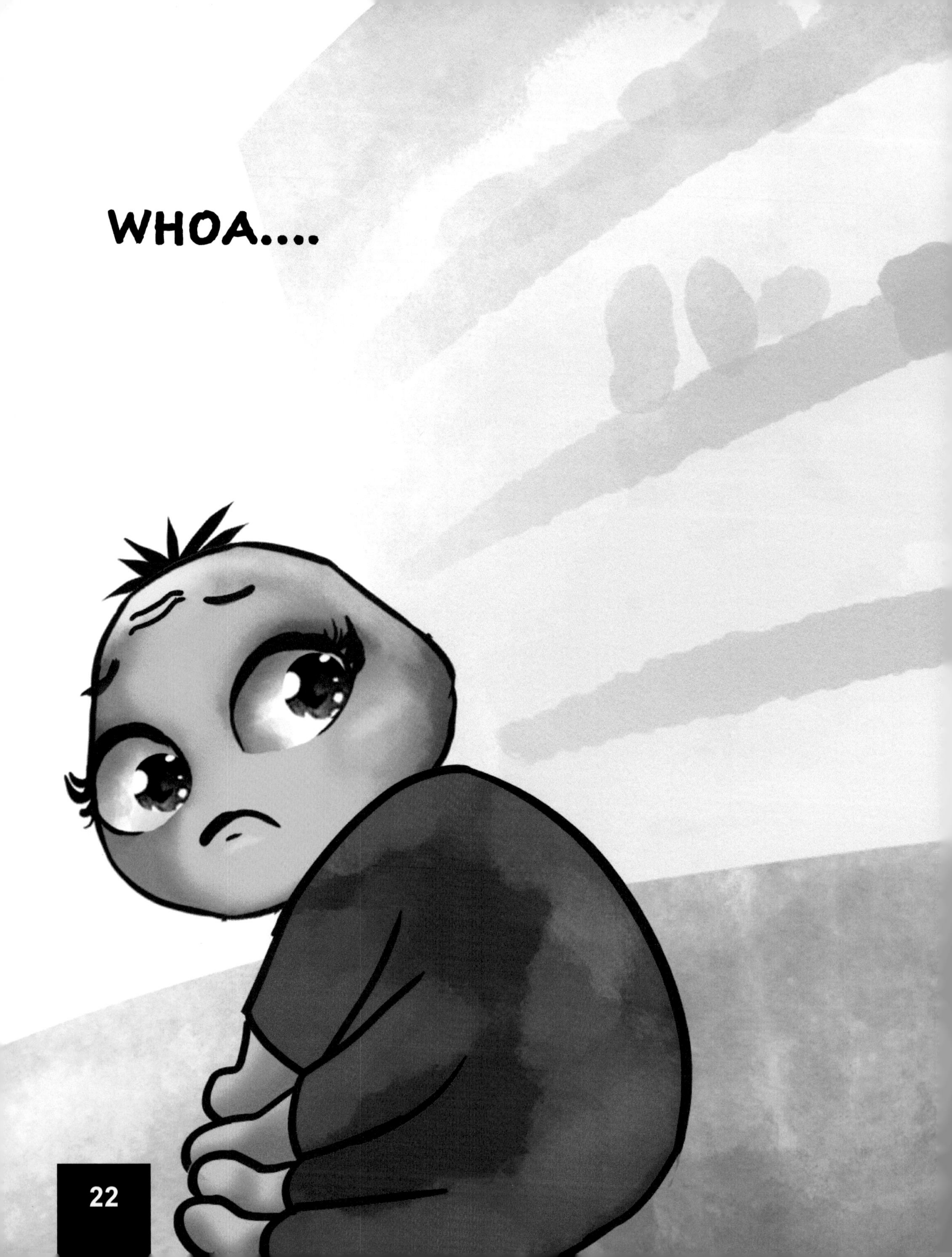
WHOA....

Itsy Bitsy did feel hating feelings toward Mama. Yet, she also loved Mama and needed Mama to love her back. Itsy Bitsy was afraid that Mama might be so angry she'd stop loving Itsy Bitsy and leave her right there on the shoe store floor - FOREVER.

Itsy Bitsy saw Mama take a deep breath.

Wow, you're FURIOUS. Let's take a few minutes to breathe and calm down.

24

Mama sat down just close enough for Itsy Bitsy to feel her love.

Following Mama's lead, Itsy Bitsy took a deep breath and filled her belly with air. She breathed deeply for several minutes and paid attention to the feeling of her breath moving through her belly.

Then Mama spoke to Itsy Bitsy about all the things that happened that day and the many confusing feelings that felt so big inside her.

The ride down the waterspout was exciting and scary. You lost your favorite shoes and we chased them so far, but we failed to save them all. You thought you were lost and alone. You were so disappointed when we couldn't get the same shoes as the ones you lost. Your feet are growing bigger, because you are growing older. It's exciting to grow up, and it's a little sad and scary. You realized that even though I can do a lot, I can't fix everything. You're exhausted...and we forgot to eat lunch. You must be starving!

As she sat on the shoe store floor talking with Mama, Itsy Bitsy felt a little stronger, a little braver, and even a little more grown up.

And that's when she saw them. They were the coolest pair of shoes she'd ever seen. Still a little embarrassed about her earlier meltdown, she softly told Mama,

I kind of like those rainbow shoes....

The next day...

The Itsy Bitsy Spider climbed up the waterspout;

Down came the rain and washed the spider out;

Out came the sun and dried up all the rain;

And the Itsy Bitsy spider climbed up the spout again...

...in her brand new rainbow shoes!

A Guide for Parents, Caregivers, and Educators

The Untold Story of Itsy Bitsy's Long, Emotional Day can be used to help identify and normalize difficult feelings, initiate dialogue about complex human experiences, and begin emotion themed discussions. Children look to grown-ups to help them cope with big feelings. They can become overloaded and dysregulated (meaning, they spiral out of control emotionally and/or behaviorally) for many reasons, including when they are tired, hungry, or overwhelmed by the bigness of their feelings. It is essential that adults create a safe atmosphere for children to talk openly about their feelings and that we avoid accidentally invalidating them, even when we don't fully understand them or wish they were different.

In the story, Mama created a safe and nurturing atmosphere by:

• taking deep breaths and staying calm herself;

• validating Itsy Bitsy's experience by acknowledging the many difficult parts of Itsy Bitsy's day and putting into words how they might have made her feel;

• connecting Itsy Bitsy's physical state (hungry and tired) to how she felt;

• staying close to Itsy Bitsy, while also giving her a little space;

• accepting Itsy Bitsy's apology.

This helped Itsy Bitsy calm down because:

• she felt understood;

• she felt loved;

• her feelings didn't feel as big and chaotic once Mama put them into words;

• her feelings felt normal;

• she knew Mama was helping her calm down;

• she took deep breaths with Mama, which helped her calm down her own body and feel more in control of herself.

It is important that like Mama, adults validate children's intense feelings, whether they are positive (such as happiness, excitement, or love) or negative (such as anger, sadness, or fear). When children are able to identify, name, and understand the numerous feelings they have, it helps them regulate their emotions and behaviors. By helping children learn the words that describe how and why they feel what they do, we help foster the development of their emotional intelligence.

Below are some discussion starters that you can use with your child. It is important for you to think about y*our own responses* to the discussion starters below, as this will model for your child how to reflect thoughtfully about experiences and feelings. Be open to what your child has to say—there are no right or wrong responses. Be curious, listen, and be supportive of your child's thoughts and feelings.

Discussion Starters that Grownups Can Use with Children

We all feel lots of different feelings and there are a lot of words that describe feelings. Let's think of some of them right now.

Itsy Bitsy felt scared when she was lost in the garden. Everybody feels scared sometimes, even grown-ups. Let's think about times when we've each felt scared. What comforts you when you are scared?

Everyone feels angry sometimes, even at people they love. Let's think about some times when we've felt really angry with someone we've loved.

Why do you think Itsy Bitsy yelled, "I hate you!" at Mama? How do you think Itsy Bitsy felt right before she said that? How do you think she felt after she said it?

When we don't get what we want or things don't turn out the way we want, we often feel disappointed. That can feel like mad and sad all mixed up. Do you remember some times when you felt disappointed? Tell me about them.

When we have big feelings, it often helps if we step back and take some deep breaths to calm down, just like Itsy Bitsy and Mama did in the story. Would you like to practice taking some deep breaths with me right now? Let's pay attention to our bellies as they rise and fall while we breathe in and out. We can pretend our bellies are balloons filling up with air when we breathe in, and then emptying when we breathe out. Let's do this 10 times.

Itsy Bitsy took deep breaths and listened to Mama speak calmly about all the big feelings she was having. This helped her feel calmer because she knew Mama understood her many emotions and they didn't feel so big and overwhelming anymore. In fact, they made sense! Let's think together about things that help us feel better when we're upset.

Even though Itsy Bitsy got so angry that she yelled, "I hate you!" at Mama, Mama still helped her calm down and helped her think about how she was feeling. Itsy Bitsy saw that she and Mama could survive her big and difficult feelings, and that they both still loved each other. Feeling Mama's love and respect helped Itsy Bitsy feel calm and in control of herself. This helped her feel more grown up, more confident, and even a little proud. Let's think of some things we've done that we feel proud about.

These are just a few conversation starters to get you and your child talking about emotions. After you use some of these examples, now you can come up with some questions of your own.

Happy reading!

Dr. Jill

To reach Dr. Leibowitz, please email her through her publisher, Wordeee at contact@wordeee.com